l'évêque doit avoir une espèce de crosse -

Reynard the Fox

Adapted from a classic folk tale and

Illustrated by Alain Vaës

Turner Publishing, Inc.

ATLANTA

Published by Turner Publishing, Inc.

A Subsidiary of Turner Broadcasting System, Inc.

1050 Techwood Drive, N.W.

Atlanta, Georgia 30318

First Edition 10 9 8 7 6 5 4 3 2 1

Library of Congress Cataloging-in-Publication Data

Vaës, Alain.

Reynard the Fox / adapted from an ancient French folk tale and illustrated by Alain Vaës. —

1st ed.

p. cm.

Summary: As he listens to a hermit recount the adventures and schemes of the wily and cunning Reynard,

a king finds a solution to a troubling dilemma.

ISBN 1-57036-055-3

1. Reynard the Fox (Legendary character) [1. Reynard the Fox (Legendary character) 2. Folklore—France. 3. Foxes—Folklore.]

I. Vaës, Alain, ill. II. Title.

PZ8. 1. V34Re 1994

398.24'52974442—dc20   94-8364

CIP

AC

Distributed by Andrews and McMeel

A Universal Press Syndicate Company

4900 Main Street

Kansas City, Missouri 64112

Printed in the U.S.A.

CAST OF CHARACTERS

King Harold

Queen Caroline

The hermit

IN THE TALE OF REYNARD

King Noble	Chanticleer the rooster
The Queen	Willie the weasel
Reynard the fox	Bruin the bear
Isegrim the wolf	Ermelyne, Reynard's wife
Courtois the poodle	Bellyn the ram
Tybalt the cat	Lop the hare
Bernard the donkey	Castor the beaver
Greybeard the badger	Dame Ruckenaw the ape

LONG AGO IN A FARAWAY KINGDOM, young Prince Harold and his beautiful bride, Caroline, were crowned king and queen. Knights and ladies, bishops and merchants, nobles and common folk—subjects from all corners of the realm—came to Court for the coronation. Everyone happily joined in the celebration—everyone, that is, but the new king.

"Why are you so sad?" asked Queen Caroline.

Young Harold sighed. "I am not ready to be king," he answered. "I have not earned the wisdom to rule. There are many in this kingdom who do not listen to me, who even covet my throne. My new subjects are greedy and constantly fight among themselves. And I am distressed that I don't know how to deal with them, how to rule them wisely. What am I to do?"

Queen Caroline understood her husband's misgivings and thought for some time before she said, "I have heard stories of someone who may be able to help us."

"Give me his name," said King Harold.

"I do not know his name," answered the queen. "But I have been told there is a wise hermit who lives among wild animals in a cave deep in the forest. Many seek him out for advice on matters simple and grave. No one knows where he comes from, how long he has been in the forest, or how he gained his wisdom. But it is known for certain that he has helped many of our subjects."

"My queen, you are very clever!" said the king. "Summon this mysterious hermit to our court."

While waiting, King Harold decided to bring all of his feuding subjects together for a feast of

reconciliation at the castle. Queen Caroline quickly sent a messenger to seek out the hermit, but he wandered back and forth through dark forests for many days before finding the cave of this wise man.

"I never expected I'd ever be invited back to Court," said the hermit, half to himself, after he had listened to the story of the troubled young king. However, he knew he could be of help, so he accompanied the messenger back to the castle. The king and queen were very relieved when the hermit arrived, while the feast was still going on, but they could not get him to remove his hood.

"We have heard you are a very wise man," said King Harold, who then proceeded to confide in the hermit all his misgivings about suddenly becoming the ruler of such unruly subjects. "Can you reveal to me the secrets of being a good king?"

"The secrets will come to you, by and by, more easily than you think," the hermit gently told the distraught king "But let me tell you a story about another king in another kingdom who had problems worse than yours and how he learned to solve them."

9

IT WAS DURING the Feast of
Whitsuntide. Spring was in flower, trees
and grasses were budding green, and the
valleys echoed with the songs of birds and
crickets. It was a time of new beginnings and a
time to seek justice and forgiveness.

King Noble looked at all this beauty and
sighed because everything else was not as perfect.
He wanted to rid his kingdom of the unhappi-
ness, injustice, and cruelty that afflicted its citi-
zens. Summoning his subjects to Court, he
decided to hear their grievances. The king and
his Council would judge once and for all who
should be punished and who should be forgiven.
Male and female, feathered, finned, and furred,
animals with two feet and those with four—
everyone responded to the royal decree. Only
one animal dared defy the king's order. It was
Reynard the fox, whose crafty deeds were
already well known throughout the land.

Sir Isegrim the wolf was the first to step up before the king to demand justice. He bowed respectfully and said, "Most gracious lord and king! You always hear our complaints and judge them fairly. I beg your lordship to hear me now. That rascal fox, Reynard, long ago my good friend, has now harmed three of my children with his dirty tricks. My desire for justice haunts me day and night!"

Isegrim was hardly finished with his complaint before Courtois the poodle had joined in. "When the snow was too deep for anyone to hunt last winter," the poodle whined, "I gladly gave to my neighbors all the food I had stored away for my own needs. I kept only a single sausage to tide me over for goodness knows how long! And, would you believe it, my last little scrap of food was stolen out of my cupboard by that sneak, Reynard!"

Before the king could respond, Sir Tybalt the cat pounced up before him and began to

wail, too, about Reynard. This whining and
howling was even more loudly interrupted by
Bernard the donkey, who brayed, "Let's not
waste the Court's time! We all know Reynard's
deeds are foul. Nothing is sacred to him. The
king could die of starvation, the entire realm
could waste away, and that fox would not
change his ways as long as *he* had enough to

eat. He should be sentenced to death for his misdeeds against the entire kingdom!"

"Right," snarled Isegrim. "While that wretched fox lives among us, there will be no peace for honest, loyal folk like us!"

One of Reynard's few friends, Greybeard the badger, spoke up for him. "You must be fair, Courtois," he said, "since you stole that very sausage from Tybalt in the first place. And Isegrim, I'm surprised at you. Many here today remember that cold winter day when you and Reynard got together to trick the driver of a wagon load of fish. Reynard was to lie in the road and pretend he was dead. When the driver saw his thick red fur in the road and thought of what a warm winter

cap it would make, he stopped quickly and threw the 'lifeless' Reynard into the back of his wagon. The clever fox then slyly tossed the fish out to you on the road while the driver continued on his way. And as fast as he threw them out, you, Isegrim, gobbled them up. When Reynard finally jumped off to collect his share, everything had been eaten except the heads and bones! I'd hardly call *your* behavior honorable, Isegrim. Reynard risked his life to share those fish with you!

"My king," Greybeard continued on, "For many months now Reynard has been living a quiet life. He even passes half the day reading books. Water is his only drink, and he eats nothing but vegetables. He gave up meat because he cannot bear the thought of bloodshed. If only he could be here today, we would all believe his innocence."

Suddenly a mournful cry shattered the sky. Everyone turned to see Chanticleer the rooster marching into Court with his family. Among them they carried the body of Greyleg, Chanticleer's favorite daughter. It was a sad, sad sight: the stately rooster leading the procession, his head bowed, his splendid robe trailing in the dirt, and the whole family crying and clucking behind him.

Chanticleer stopped before the king and tried three times to put his grief into words, but each time he was so overcome he could not speak. Finally, after managing a long, shrill crow, he said, "Hail, sovereign king, before you lies a victim of that cruel fox, Reynard. This poor innocent soul, my beloved daughter, was slain within her convent yard by the despicable Reynard, disguised in the robes of a holy monk. Save us from him, please, before my entire family shares her fate."

In the crowd, Willie the weasel, who was not the only one there to admire the fox's cleverness, murmured to his neighbors, "You know, my friends, it is only a fox's true nature to hunt chickens and smaller animals. I only wish that I was as sharp as he is, to always get away with everything, as he does!" Others in the crowd nodded in agreement.

The king, who had listened patiently to all the complaints and had not said a word till now, stood up with fire in his eyes. Angrily, he turned to the badger and commanded, "Come hither, sir, to see this example of your friend Reynard's work! Quiet life, indeed. I cannot allow this wretched creature to go unpunished. He must be brought before us to face his accusers."

Since no one seemed eager to be the one to summon this crafty criminal to Court, the king and Council chose Sir Bruin the bear to do this job. The king warned Sir Bruin, "Beware, my friend, this fox is ruthless and cunning."

"Fear not, my noble king," the burly Bruin boasted. "No miserable little fox can outwit this knight!"

So Sir Bruin strode purposefully through forests and over mountains until he reached Reynard's castle, Malepartus. Standing outside the gate, the bear bellowed, "Ho, Reynard, it is Bruin the bear! I have been specially sent by our sovereign king to bring you back to stand trial for your many grievous wrongdoings."

Reynard opened his door for the bear and said warmly, "Welcome, dearest Bruin. Of course I shall accompany you back to Court. I have nothing to fear there. But first come inside and rest the night; you look worn out." He added, "My wife, Ermelyne, and I have little food worthy of such an honored guest, but I know where you might find some honey, if you care for that sort of thing."

"Honey!" exclaimed the bear, his stomach growling. "Oh, but that is my favorite food." Completely forgetting the purpose of his visit, the hungry bear followed the fox into the woods.

"Be careful! You must not disturb the bees," warned the fox as he led Sir Bruin to an old fallen oak tree. A woodcutter's wedge had been driven into the tree trunk, so it could be split into firewood. The fox pointed to the gap the wedge had opened and said, "There's more honey deep in there than you could ever hope to eat."

Bruin's tummy got the best of his head and he greedily thrust his arm into the gap in the tree, up to his shoulder. The conniving fox then yanked out the wedge and the opening snapped shut, locking poor Bruin's entire arm in the tree and yanking his face up against its trunk! Howling with pain, Bruin twisted and turned, but he could not manage to free himself. In fact he did himself even more harm as he swung the trunk back and forth, crashing it into other trees. Finally he tore his arm out of the tree trunk, leaving much of his fur behind. Blinded by pain, Bruin crashed and dashed about wildly

until he fell right into the river. So miserable
was he that gladly he would have drowned in
the deep water. Instead, the swift current kept
him afloat, finally dumping his bruised body
ashore way downstream.

"Reynard," he moaned into the dirt. "You are
a vile traitor. I will have revenge, I swear!"

It took poor Bruin four days to stagger home.
When the king saw the great beast he cried,
"Good heavens! Is this the noble Sir Bruin?"

"Yes," declared the bear. "And this is what that treacherous fox does to royal messengers!"

"This is an outrage!" shouted the king. "By my crown, I swear, justice will be done."

King Noble called his Council, and all decided to send another messenger to summon Reynard. The king gave this honor to Tybalt the cat.

"My king," wailed the cat. "Pray tell me how I might succeed at persuading that ruthless fox to come when I am so very small and even the mighty Bruin failed?"

"You may not be a giant," said the king, "but your wisdom and wit will make up for your small size."

The poor cat bowed his head and accepted the assignment, but he begged the king for an official summons to present Reynard. Tybalt then took the royal decree directly to Malepartus, where he found Reynard sitting outside the gate.

"Good evening," said Tybalt. "I bring a stern warning from the king. If you do not return to Court with me, you and your entire family will have to pay with your lives."

Reynard smiled and said, "Of course I'll come with you. But first let's have some supper. Then you should rest, and we will start off first thing in the morning."

The smart cat countered quickly. "As a matter of fact, I think we should start back tonight."

"Heavens, no," said the fox. "One can never tell what kind of cutthroats and thieves one might meet on the road at night."

"Maybe you're right," agreed Tybalt. "What will you serve for supper if we stay the night?"

"Would a tender morsel of country mouse suit your fancy?" asked Reynard.

"Oh, my, yes," said the cat, licking his chops and flexing out his sharp claws.

"I know where you can have a sumptuous feast," said Reynard, as he led the hungry Tybalt to the parson's barn. Now, in the side of the barn was a hole Reynard had cut for himself the day before, when he stole a chicken, so he took the unsuspecting Tybalt right to that

very same hole! When the cat heard the sounds of dozens of mice scurrying around inside the barn, he pounced through the opening. But before he knew it, a rope noose had yanked tight around his neck! Snatched off his feet, Tybalt did a somersault in midair as the rope tightened. He began to thrash around, but he only made the noose tighter.

Reynard snickered. Just as he had suspected, the parson's clever little nephew had set a trap for him, to catch him the next time he came by for a free chicken dinner.

As the cat struggled helplessly and clawed at the noose, Reynard asked out loud, "Dear Tybalt, are you perhaps eating too fast? I hope you aren't choking on those fat and tasty morsels!"

By now the commotion in the barn had woken the nimble nephew, who jumped out of bed, thinking he had finally caught the wily fox. When he saw it was only poor Tybalt in his trap, the nephew whacked the cat on the head and left him for dead.

Reynard, who had been watching from the woods, smirked that each blow Tybalt received was really meant for him. "You shouldn't have been so greedy or careless, clever cat!"

Tybalt, though battered and bruised, was not

dead, and he used every last ounce of strength to chew through the rope around his neck. After freeing himself, the wounded Tybalt stumbled back down the road to Court, swearing revenge on the wicked fox.

King Noble, who had been forced to seek out poor Tybalt in the hospital, for his report on Reynard, was enraged to find him so badly done by. The king and his Council then and there condemned Reynard to death for his vile deeds.

"PRAY CEASE IMMEDIATELY, old hermit," demanded King Harold. "King Noble has proved no better than I in dealing with evil-doers. Just as in this kingdom, the innocent suffer and the wicked prosper. How will King Noble ever bring justice and happiness to his people? What can I possibly learn from this story, old hermit?"

"Surely, wise hermit," Queen Caroline bitterly interjected. "You don't intend to suggest that good King Harold model himself on that despicable fox?"

"Be patient, your royal highnesses, and hear me out," said the hermit. "You will find that wisdom often comes to you from depths you least expected you had."

Bᴜᴛ Gʀᴇʏʙᴇᴀʀᴅ ᴛʜᴇ Bᴀᴅɢᴇʀ was
not easily persuaded of his old friend's guilt and
pleaded once more on the fox's behalf.
"Remember, my king, what your just laws stipu-
late, that one must be summoned and fail to
appear three times before one can be condemned."

"Who," asked the discouraged king, "would be
foolish enough to try to summon Reynard a
third time?"

"I will," answered the badger. "If you allow
me to be your royal messenger."

"So be it," said the king.

The badger then made haste for Malepartus,
where he tried to reason with Reynard. "This is
your third summons," said the badger. "If you
delay further, the king and his Council will
come here and destroy you, your family, and
Malepartus."

Fully confident he could still outwit anyone

alive, the fox agreed to follow Greybeard back. Word quickly spread that Reynard was on his way to Court, and everyone rushed outside, eager to get a glimpse of the famous scoundrel.

At last, the fearless fox stood before the king and said, "My lord, I am—and have always been—one of your most loyal, and least understood, servants. And I welcome your invitation to defend myself against the outrageous accusations my enemies have made behind my back."

"Silence!" cried the king. "How dare you lie about your loyalty? We have all seen how cruelly you treat my subjects."

"But, good king," said the fox. "You judge only by what others have told you. Can you really blame me for Bruin's comeuppance when he so wrongly tried to steal the woodcutter's honey? Or when Tybalt so foolishly attempted to eat the parson's mice? Did I lay a hand on them?"

"How malicious a mongrel you are! What about the evil you've done to Isegrim's family and poor Chanticleer's favorite daughter?" demanded the king. Before Reynard could even reply, the Council had pronounced him guilty and had him led straight to the gallows.

But the wily fox didn't give up so easily. He piously begged King Noble for a just moment

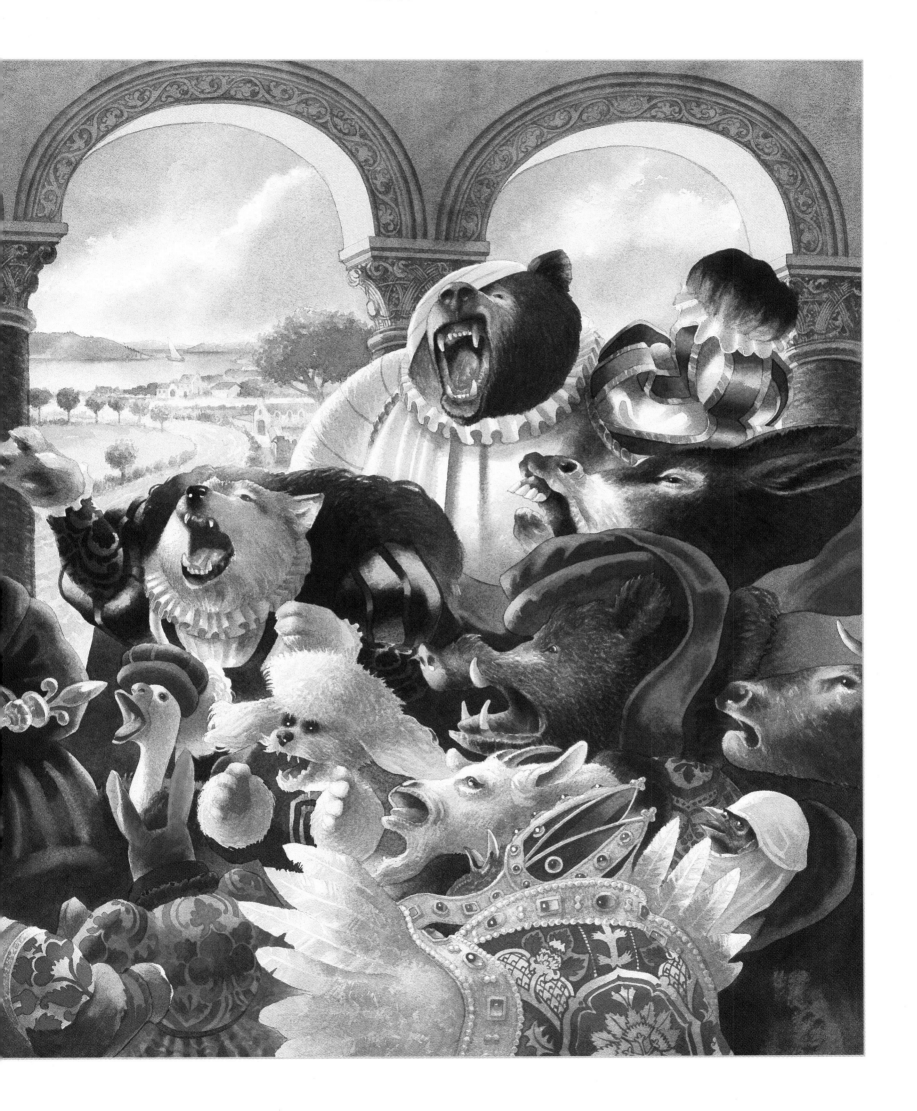

to clear his conscience, to confess his many sins before he was hanged. The king, who had a good heart, could not deny him this.

Reynard took great care in thanking the king for his kindness and humbly announced, "I'll never lie to you, your highness." The words were hardly out of his mouth before he began to confess that maybe he had made a few mistakes and had, indeed, stolen a few things in his life, but nothing compared to the treasure his father had made off with. He mumbled on and on about the wagon loads of gold and silver and precious gems his father had accumulated. Reynard sensed that the only way he could possibly survive this crisis was to prey upon the collective greed of the assembled courtiers.

As King Noble tried to sort out this bewildering tale, his queen began to daydream about the piles of gold and silver and precious gems.

"What happened to this wonderful treasure?" she asked.

"It is hidden well," said Reynard. "My wife, Ermelyne, and I have pledged never to reveal its whereabouts, for we've heard that there are those in this kingdom who might use it wrongfully to hire an army and overthrow our beloved king."

When the queen motioned for Reynard to

come closer, there was a little stir as many of the king's loyal subjects coughed nervously, glanced around, or stared at the ground.

"Surely," she whispered, "no one we know would ever want to overthrow our generous king. Your secret is safe with us."

"Why should I tell you what I know?" asked the fox. "You haven't believed a word I've said."

"It's another trick!" said the king.

"But what if it is not?" said the queen. "If the secret dies with the fox, we will surely lose the treasure, and maybe even the kingdom. If, however, you pardon him, he could lead us to this great treasure so that no one else can find it and harm us."

Reluctantly the king gave in to her wishes and pardoned the fox. "But this is the last time I will trust you, Reynard. Believe me, you will regret it if this is another one of your vile tricks! Now lead us to your so-called treasure."

The fox, of course, could never take them to these imaginary riches, so he continued stalling. "My king, to prove that my remorse is genuine, I beg you to let me make a pilgrimage to Rome to receive the Pope's pardon. But the treasure is so well hidden that even I need a map to find it. I will be glad to go home and bring it to you."

The king and queen, out of greed, foolishly

believed Reynard once more. Noble then ordered both Lop the hare and Bellyn the ram to accompany Reynard back to Malepartus to get the map before the fox departed for Rome.

"Stay together!" the king warned Lop and Bellyn. "Two will have a better chance than one against this crafty fox."

The three finally arrived at Malepartus. Lop was tired and Bellyn was hungry, so Reynard encouraged Bellyn to stay outside the castle gate and enjoy some of the luscious pasture grasses. "Meanwhile, Lop can rest inside while I go find the map," he suggested.

Thus, despite the king's warning, the hare and the ram were separated, and the innocent Lop was soon roasted for Reynard's dinner. The fox took the rabbit's fur, sealed it in a pouch, and carried it out to Bellyn, who was still happily munching in the pasture. "The hare is quite exhausted from our journey," said Reynard. "But you are now refreshed, so why don't you go on without him. The king is anxious for this map and will reward you for your diligence. As soon as the hare has rested, my wife will make him a hearty meal, and we will send him after you.

"But do not dare try to open this pouch," he added. "The knots are tied in such a way that King Noble will know if you have tampered with his treasure map." Reynard was certain that when the king realized that he and his subjects had been outwitted even once more, they'd never dare bother him again.

As the ram hurried back to Court, he congratulated himself for being the bearer of such important papers and took the pouch straight to his king.

"The treasure map, my lord," said the ram, as he offered up the bag. "Reynard could not wait to get it to his beloved king, so I decided, on my own, to come ahead without Lop."

King Noble called for Castor the beaver to help undo the knots. When the strings were untied, Castor put his hand into the pouch and, to his surprise, pulled out Lop's fur!

The Court was horrified beyond belief. King Noble cried out, "Oh, Lop! Lop!" Then the mighty sovereign lowered his head and wept.

"Oh, how severely have we been deceived yet once more," he moaned. "It is Reynard who rules this realm, not me! Never again will this traitor play his tricks on me!"

The king decided once and for all to put an end to Reynard's ceaseless conniving. If he continued to let his subjects see Reynard get away with all manner of evil deeds, how could he expect Willie the weasel and Greybeard to stop admiring the wily ways of that artful fox? "To Malepartus," he shouted. "We'll storm the villain's castle and hang him without another word."

Once near Malepartus, Isegrim the wolf approached the king, "For all our grievances, let me, the fiercest of the fierce, challenge this fox to single combat, unto death!"

"I have complete faith in you, brave Isegrim," said King Noble. "But you know the Code of Combat as well as I. If, under such a challenge, Reynard should win—even by one of his roguish tricks—I am bound to forgive him his

wrongs and restore all rights to him."

"Fear not, my king," boasted Isegrim. "That fox will never get the better of me again!"

After some hesitation, the king decided to permit Isegrim to challenge the fox. It would be one last chance to show the secret admirers of Reynard that his crafty way of life had led to his undoing. "Let the battle begin at dawn," he announced to the Council and to his armies.

That night, at Malepartus, clever old Dame Ruckenaw the ape pulled Reynard aside and whispered advice into his ear. She would shave him from head to bottom—everything but his tail! Then she would smear his body and tail with fats and oils, so that when he and Isegrim fought it would be impossible for the wolf to get a firm hold on him.

"The first thing you must do in battle," the
ape said, "is to drag your oily tail back and
forth through the dirt and sand until it is well
covered in grit. Then, as soon as you can find
the opportunity, you must whip your tail into
the wolf's face. When he stops to wipe his
blinded eyes, Isegrim will be at your mercy!
Victory will be within your grasp."

At sunrise the next morning the two combat-
ants appeared before the king and queen.
Following the ape's advice, Reynard dragged his
oily tail back and forth in the sand. But before
the referee even finished reading the rules aloud,
the snarling Isegrim had lunged at Reynard.
However, each time Isegrim thought he had the

fox in his grip, Reynard slithered out of his clutches.

Finally Reynard saw his chance. He hit Isegrim directly in the eyes with his tail, and, indeed, the wolf was temporarily blinded. Seeing his opening, the fox then leapt at the wolf. Gripping Isegrim by the throat, with his very sharp teeth, he snarled, "If you humbly call me your lord and master, I will spare your life. If not, I will close my jaws around your throat."

The proud wolf could not face the humiliation and gave himself up for dead, but the king halted the fight before it went any further.

"Enough," declared the king. "Reynard is the victor." Exhausted by all his efforts and unable to get up, the fox looked over at the blinded wolf, his good friend of years before. He used to go hunting with Isegrim all the time, and, yet, a few minutes ago this wolf had actually tried to kill him! How had it come about that good friends were now deadly enemies? Was it all his fault, as the king had said? Was what he had been warned about so many times really true, that his tricky ways would eventually lead to his own undoing? What if Dame Ruckenaw had not given him such good advice, would the outcome of this battle have been very much different? Reynard decided that he had better

go away for a while and give all of this a lot more thought. His luck *could* run out!

Reynard staggered to his feet and bowed to his king and the Council. The sovereign, reluctantly abiding by his kingdom's Code of Combat, pardoned the fox, restoring all privileges of citizenship and former power.

"Furthermore," the king unexpectedly went on. "In recognition of your supreme cleverness, I now appoint you Lord High Chancellor of the Animal Kingdom. As such, you will perform a very special, though dangerous mission as our first ambassador to the humans' world. But, to succeed at this, as you do in every undertaking, you must leave here immediately to dwell forever on the outskirts of mankind's villages and towns. You have proved to us more than once that no other animal can match your cleverness and craft, so it is our royal pride in you as one of us to send you forth to demonstrate to the humans that animals can match wits with them and even teach them a trick or two."

Reynard, a bit stunned by this turn of events, studied the king's face for a long moment, marveling at the new look of confidence and satisfaction in his eyes. Then, with a puzzled smile, Reynard bowed deeply before his sovereign.

"I accept the great honor," he responded.

"So," KING HAROLD SAID, "the way to justly rule a kingdom is to diligently weed out bad influences from the start. How clever of King Noble to learn this and finally to outwit the wily fox by playing upon his overweening pride. Old hermit, as you promised, this has been a very good lesson for me."

"Well, it could have ended differently," the hermit quickly pointed out. "That sharp fox certainly was not at his wit's end, but events of those few days weighed heavily upon him. Although he knew it was his nature to be clever and to survive by hunting other animals, he had never given much thought to what harm his actions had done others. He had not been a good neighbor, it was true. Yet, it was not really in his nature to be one. So he decided to avoid ever harming anyone else by settling all alone in a cave far away from everyone. Over years, the wiser Reynard was able to help those who sought him out, for he had plenty of time to think through the world's problems."

"How do you know so much about Reynard's thoughts?" Queen Caroline asked.

"You will have to trust me," said the old hermit, as he turned and headed back to his distant cave in the dark forest.

COLOPHON

WALTON RAWLS—Vice President, Editorial

KATHERINE BUTTLER—Editor

ELIZABETH ISELE—Writer

MICHAEL WALSH—Vice President, Design

ELAINE STREITHOF—Book Design

ANNE MURDOCH—Production Manager

❧

TITLE TREATMENT by Kelly Hume

❧

CONTRIBUTORS TO THE TEXT:

Alain Vaës, Elizabeth Isele, Larry Larson, Katherine Buttler, Walton Rawls,

and special thanks to Lincoln Kirstein for suggesting REYNARD to the artist.

❧

Typefaces used are Koch Antiqua and Snell Roundhand

Color separations by Graphics International, Atlanta, Georgia

Printed by Horowitz-Rae Book Manufacturers, Fairfield, New Jersey

on Sterling Satin.